MW00980780

Eagle Feather

Eagle Feather

by Sonia Gardner
artwork by James R. Spurlock

published by
Writers Press

DEDICATION

James and I wish to express our gratitude to Liz Mummey and the Native American Coalition of Boise for their guidance. We would also like to thank the Native American community for allowing us the privilege of using a Native American theme.

Last we wish to thank family and friends for their love and support, with a special thanks to Bill and Lynda for their never ending patience and encouragement and to Yogi for his partnership.

INTRODUCTION

Native Americans have a historically rich culture that encourages individuals to discover the inner strengths they possess. These strengths enable us to meet life's challenges. The culture also teaches respect and an appreciation for all life. I found all these qualities to be the perfect backdrop for Eagle Feather's story.

Everyone experiences blindness of some kind; whether it be physical or through prejudice. How we meet these challenges and learn from them is what matters. This lesson is the message in Eagle Feather, the story of a young Native American blind boy who uses the talking stick to represent the strengths he needs to help meet life's challenges. With his courage, he helps everyone see beyond their own blindness and realize the gifts that each of us possess.

I hope you enjoy the message and the chance to experience Eagle Feather's world.

Sonia Gardner

The day of the Naming Ceremony was here – the day Little One would get a new name. All the elders would gather around the fire to discuss Little One's coming into manhood. They would give him a new name honoring his Vision Quest.

Little One, sightless from birth, had prepared a special talking stick to be used at the ceremony. It was his way of representing the strengths he valued, and to remind the speaker to always speak strong and true. Everyone there must listen with respect, to the person holding the stick.

Little One chose a small piece of rabbit pelt, which represented listening, to place upon his talking stick. Then he placed a part of an elk's antler, which represented strength, upon the stick.

Last of all he added a tail feather of a hawk. The feather was important to Little One, for it represented truth.

Little One's excitement was growing. The most important night of his life was about to begin.

The sun's warmth slowly faded from Little One's cheek. A chill filled the night air.

The elders gathered around the ceremonial fire. Little One heard the strong voice of Running Horse. It overpowered everyone in the circle. He felt Running Horse disliked him, but did not understand the reason.

All became quiet except the soft rumble of the drums. As Little One listened to their rhythm, he remembered his Vision Quest.

He had prepared for the Quest by enduring the purification ceremony. He recalled the hot, moist sensation of the sweat lodge.

The day after the purification, he began his Vision Quest with the blessings of his grandfather and the support of his companion Gray Wolf. Gray Wolf had been Little One's trusted friend and guide since Little One was three years old.

On that warm summer morning, Gray Wolf led the way up the trail. Little One smelled huckleberries and wild onions. He heard the water trickle gently. He knew the pool where he had fished with Grandfather was close by.

Gray Wolf stopped by a tall tree. Little One could feel the markings on the tree that he had found a few summers ago. He knew this was the place. He gathered rocks and made his sacred circle. He sat in the middle of it.

Two sunrises had passed when Little One heard the cry of an eagle. In his Vision he saw it. The eagle spoke to him and told him about the special gifts he possessed. As the eagle disappeared it dropped a feather.

Little One felt the eagle's feather beside his feet. He knew it was time to go back.

He remembered the excitement he felt that morning as he held the feather in his hands.

Little One was awakened from his memories by the sudden silence of the drums. He heard the Chief's voice. "Today before us," the Chief began, "at the age of manhood, is the boy we call Little One. He is a survivor of the great War. Battles fought bravely by many. Battles that took his parents, Black Beaver and Spotted Fawn."

14

"Tonight we honor their memory by remembering their son." The Chief gently touched Little One's shoulder and continued, "He is a child born into the world before his time, small and without sight. He stands before you now, and asks to become a man. Shall we give him a name that symbolizes bravery and power?"

The Elders began to talk among themselves. One of them stood. Holding the talking stick, Running Horse spoke strong words.

"What can this blind boy do? What use is he to the tribe?"

Sharp pain pierced Little One's heart. He felt a lump in his throat, but he knew he must be brave. He hoped they would realize his blindness did not make him a lesser man. He must ignore the hurtful words of Running Horse.

17

Another Elder stood. Taking the stick, he spoke in a soft, familiar voice. "Is it not true that Little One knows first when the rain will fall to water our corn? Or warns us when the snow will fall so we may gather and prepare for winter? Does he not smell the rain and snow?"

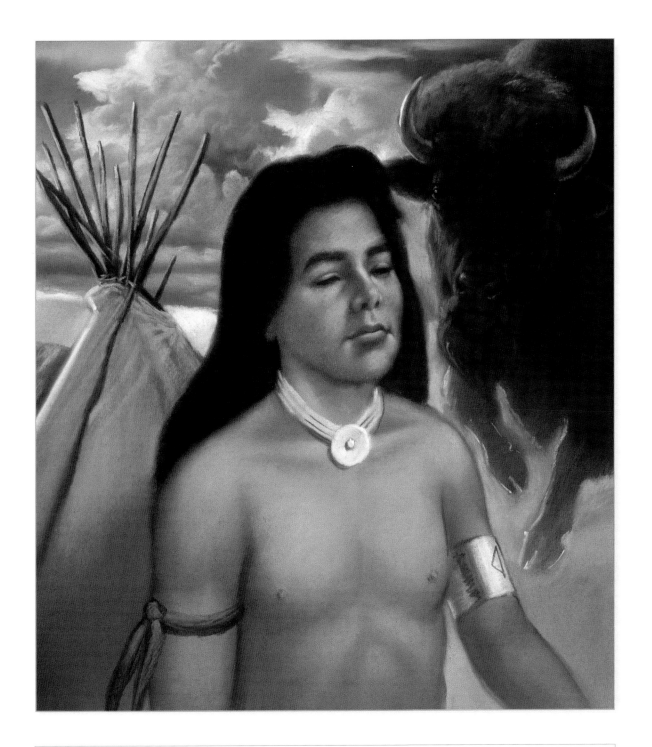

Little One smiled at the gentle voice of his grandfather, Broken Arrow.

"Little One can smell and feel when the mighty buffalo will cross our path," Broken Arrow continued, "and when the winds tell us that we must seek shelter. The Great One has given him many gifts."

20

Running Horse wished to speak again. Broken Arrow passed him the stick.

"But can he hunt or provide for a family?" Running Horse asked.

Taking back the stick, Broken Arrow replied, "Yes, Little One has successfully hunted birds and rabbits and has caught fish from the river."

"He has the keen ears of a deer, that is ready to flee at the snap of a twig."

"Yes, to flee!" interrupted Running Horse. "To flee in battle!" The angry words echoed in Little One's ears.

"Stop!" the Chief told Running Horse, "You speak out of order." Then taking a tomahawk, he turned to Broken Arrow and asked, "What of battle?"

"Not all warriors go to battle," said Broken Arrow. "In the war council we need those who can see beyond the fight. The eagle visited Little One in his Vision and gave him a feather. Is it not the eagle who sees with clarity and sharpness, those things which we cannot see?"

"Much like the eagle, Little One possesses the power and wisdom about things we cannot see. These are his special gifts. Therefore, I, Broken Arrow, proclaim that Little One's name should be Eagle Feather, to symbolize the gifts the Great Spirit has given him."

With nods of approval, the elders awaited the Chief's words.

The Chief stood behind Little One and spoke. "Broken Arrow's words ring true. From this day on Little One will be known as Eagle Feather – One Who Sees In Darkness." The Chief gave Little One his talking stick.

Little One turned with the guiding touch of Broken Arrow and said, "Grandfather, I shall make you proud." Then one of the elders gave Little One his ceremonial vest and Broken Arrow placed the feather upon his head.

Little One used those powers we all possess to accept those things he could not see. With his courage and wisdom he would always be known as Eagle Feather, *One Who Sees In Darkness.*

And what of Running Horse?

Running Horse grew to understand and respect Eagle Feather. He learned to look beyond his own blindness and appreciate the special gifts that Eagle Feather possessed. Through their friendship Running Horse discovered the meaning of true vision – vision that can only be seen with the heart.

*True vision soars when embraced in the
enduring winds of encouragement.*

Each of us is born with a special gift.
The challenge is to discover what
that gift is.

So if each child is a gift,
then the greatest pleasure is. . .
the discovery
of what's inside.

The Author